To
Cara

THE LAST GIRLS STANDING: THE BEGINNING

L.C. Valentine

Thanks for the support.

To Kerry,

*Who always inspires me, and deserves this dedication,
even if she doesn't like any of the Friday the 13th movies.*

THE BEGINNING

Ellie felt her sneakers slip on the slick ground as she pushed. The sound of the wheels of Melissa's sporty convertible spinning in the slop filled her ears, but failed to distract from the mud splashing back onto her jeans. The car bucked and shook, but refused to budge on the muddy road leading to the camp.

'Yuck!' Ellie announced out loud, jumping back, away from the rear of the car and almost losing her balance as she slid on the slick surface. Melissa stopped gunning the engine, looking back at Ellie, a smile on elegantly painted pink lips beneath her perfect blonde hair.

'Aren't you going to keep pushing?' she asked in that tone of her's that suggested everybody should instantly do as she wanted, at all times.

'I've only got two pairs of jeans with me for the whole six weeks! And who knows when I'll get a chance to wash them!' Ellie protested in irritation, looking down at her mud splattered pants.

'You only brought *two* pairs of jeans for the entire trip?' Melissa raised one of her perfectly sculpted eyebrows. Ellie shot her a look, but bit back on commenting on how not *all* of them had closets the size of small cities like Melissa to carry infinite clothes.

'The car's probably only stuck because it's weighed down with all those cases you insisted on bringing.' she opted for instead, deciding it was still enough of a quip to leave her with some confidence.

'Uh, my car is just having a *little trouble*, that's all. It's not stuck! Besides, it's only because whoever is running this camp clearly has never heard of a quality road.' Melissa said snottily, and Ellie wondered if it was her imagination or if the spoiled girl had literally turned her nose into the air. Ellie sighed. The man running the camp was Billy Clarkson. Ellie knew because she actually bothered to observe what was going on around her in the world, and had read the numerous pieces of reading he had sent out prior to attending. Melissa apparently hadn't bothered, including the recommendation to only bring 4x4s to the camp as the road hadn't been paved.

'Billy said in all the information he sent out that this part of the camp hasn't been opened for *years*. We're lucky the path is still here at all.' Ellie said as she approached the front of the car, putting her hands on the hood and gesturing for Melissa to try backwards. She did so. The wheels whirred again, but as only her back wheels were spinning, this time most of the mud splatter missed Ellie. However, as hard as she pushed, the car didn't budge an inch. Of course, it didn't help that Ellie's street sneakers weren't exactly appropriate for the terrain either, and just kept slipping in the muck. They were now almost entirely brown, their bright white colour a distant memory.

'Push harder!' Melissa insisted as she looked back down the road, watching her futility spinning tires. Ellie gave up with a heavy sigh, and walked back over to the door.

'You know, you could try pushing and I could try driving?' she suggested pointedly. Melissa offered another one of her perfect pink smiles.

'When you can afford a car like this, you can *drive* a car like this.' she replied snobbily. Ellie just sighed.

Of all of her friends, Melissa was the one Ellie had been the most reluctant to travel to the camp with. It wasn't that she didn't like the blonde, it was just that she had no idea why she *did* like the blonde. Melissa was your typical, spoiled rich girl. She came from a wealthy family and had only gone to the same school as Ellie and her friends after she got kicked out of her posh private school for reasons she had never gone into. Ellie, the poor black girl from the working class single mom, had never been the type of person Melissa would like to associate with, or so Ellie assumed, and everything in Melissa's attitude reinforced that stereotype. But Melissa had latched onto Natalie, no doubt the leader of their group of friends, not to mention always popular for causing mischief in school, on her very first day and had become a regular in the group ever since.

That hadn't stopped there being a short, private Facebook private messaging discussion about who was going to be the one who had to suffer Melissa's snobby disdain for the drive to the camp. Somehow, Ellie had lost the argument on that one, and so, she had ended up trying to desperately push a hopelessly-inappropriate-for-the-terrain sports coupe out of the mud.

'I knew we should have let Danny make two trips in his jeep.' Ellie said, trying to tactfully suggest that next time maybe Melissa should *listen* to her. Technically, it wasn't a jeep, but an SUV. Ellie knew that, but she immediately called any big wheeled off road vehicle a "jeep".

'Uh, I'll be *dead* before I ride in that thing.' Melissa insisted.

'Instead, you're just stuck in the mud.' Ellie mocked a little, folding her arms. Melissa slammed her foot down on the pedal angrily, the wheels on her car whirring so madly that Ellie had to jump back to avoid being splattered by mud all over again.

'Ugh, you win. It's stuck.' Melissa sighed dramatically. 'I don't suppose you get a signal out here, do you?' she asked. Evidently, Melissa was already checking her phone with her manicured fingernails.

'No, but the camp is only about a mile away. Let's just walk down there and get Danny to come back and tow you out later. Or Billy. I bet Billy's got some rugged jeep thing too.' Ellie knew that suggesting they *walk* was risky with Melissa, who was as prissy and prone to avoiding anything strenuous as her snobby rich girl reputation suggested, but even Melissa knew she had no choice and sighed.

'Fine!' Melissa got out of the car with a dramatic flounce, wrinkling her nose as her designer sandals landed in the muck. Ellie lifted her rucksack out of the back of the car. It was weighty, but she could manage it for the short trip. Melissa seemed to consider dragging one of her suitcases, but thought better of it. Ellie figured she thought she'd get them when Danny inevitably came back to rescue her car, but judging by the mud on the road up ahead, there was no way on this Earth or any other that Melissa's expensive convertible was going to make it to the campground.

Ellie became acutely aware of the silence as the two stood there, looking up at the old sign.

ST MARY'S MARSH CAMPGROUND
WHERE THE FUN NEVER STOPS
EST. 1928

It was clearly a sign from the time the original camp had been opened, judging by its weathered appearance, and the extremely eighties faded image of some children building a tent that was made out below it, but it was neither the contents of the sign nor the age of it that had stopped the two girls in their tracks.

It was the bloody corpse of the animal that was impaled upon one of the large, broken wooden shafts that extended above the sign. The animal's innards dripped down the front of the sign, right through the middle of the world "marsh" and ironically blotting out the word "fun" nearly completely.

'Ew. Ew. Ewwwww.' Melissa fretted. 'I am *not* cleaning that up!' she insisted, folding her arms and turning away in disgust. Ellie was a little impressed. She had figured Melissa was the type to lose her lunch at the sight of such a thing. As it was, Ellie felt more queasy than she did.

'How did it get up there?' she asked, although she knew Melissa wouldn't be able to provide an answer.'

'Who cares!? It's gross! First thing we do when we get to the camp is get Danny to take it down and bury it somewhere!' Melissa insisted.

'*First?*' Ellie asked sceptically. 'You mean, before he even frees your car?' she added teasingly.

'Uh, *yeah!* I'm not driving my car past *that!*' she jabbed a hand up at the strange creature. 'What even *is* it anyway?'

'I dunno. Looks like a wolf. Maybe a coyote?' Ellie commented. 'I'm more concerned about how it got up there!' she added, a little louder than she had intended.

'Can wolves jump that high?' Melissa asked with a wrinkled nose. Ellie didn't dignify that with an answer.

'I mean, the brochure said this was bear country. Maybe… it fought a bear?' That sounded stupid as soon as it left Ellie's lips, but she had said it anyway. Melissa turned, frustrated, glaring at Ellie.

'Bears! Mud! Wolves! How did I let you talk me into this!? Do you realise cell phones don't even work in this place!?' This was classic Melissa, blaming the nearest face. It hadn't been Ellie's idea. When Billy's fliers had gone up in school, looking for camp counsellors to work at St. Mary's Marsh, the newly reopening campground, it had been *Danny* who had suggested it to the group. It would be the summer after they all graduated, he had said, and not all of them had the money for a real vacation. So why not earn some cash for college *and* spend the summer together at the campground? He had thought it had been perfect. Ellie, who was a self confessed horror movie fan, had spent far too many evenings and late nights staying up watching *Friday the 13th* and *Sleepaway Camp* marathons to ever think being a camp counsellor was a *good* idea, but she'd been talked around. As had Melissa, who hadn't liked the idea of anything that involved her having to do *work* at first.

'Don't blame me. I was happy staying at home all summer.' Ellie said instead, with a shrug. 'We'd better keep on moving. I mean, I'm no expert, but I think old blood goes dark. That blood... it's bright red.'

'Are you saying...?' Melissa trailed off.

'Yeah, whatever killed it might still be around.' Ellie gulped as she said it, and began moving towards the camp again, arms on the straps of her pack. She didn't bother to look to see if Melissa was following.

The rest of the walk was uneventful, even if Ellie found her eyes kept scanning the undergrowth for signs of a hockey masked killer about to jump out on them. Or a sackheaded killer. She wasn't biased towards *Friday the 13th Part Two* just because it didn't feature the hockey mask. She supposed that by that logic she should also be on the lookout for a disgruntled camp cook, but she had always felt confident she could take Pamela Voorhees in a fight at least. Maybe that was arrogance. It was easy to sit back and claim you could do better when watching a horror movie, she supposed.

The camp came into view almost instantly as they emerged from the undergrowth, passing beneath a wooden arch with the camp name emblazoned upon it, and Ellie realised that she would have to adjust her expectations. All of the images Billy had sent in his documentation had shown the camp in its prime, but what greeted her was anything but. The brown wooden buildings looked run down and shabby, all signs of their paint having peeled away. She could see new boards put in the roof over one of the cabins, and they stood out like a sore thumb. The windows looked new too, the frames unpainted, pale wood the colour of a milky coffee, compared to the stained, dark brown of the rest of the building. Ellie nearly tripped over a pile of wood by her feet, and glanced down, to see that it was one long wooden pole, and six flat pieces of wood shaped like quirky arrows. Each had a word written on it.

She could make out "friendship", "self-reliance", and what looked like "compassion", but the majority of the word was hidden by the pile. The rest were buried at the bottom. The wood was fresh and new, like the windows and the rooftop panel, and Ellie figured this was a welcome sign they would need to build. They had a week before the camp opened to get it into shape. Ellie had been expecting an easy week, a bit of painting, and then fun and games for the week before the kids arrived. She was realising now that she was very wrong indeed, and that there would be plenty of work to do before the week was out.

Gathered in what was a form of central square between the cabins and the large community hut, Ellie could see two jeeps, and the smattering of people. They were all talking among themselves, and hadn't yet noticed Ellie approach. Her eyes immediately went to Danny, drawn to him. The pair weren't officially dating or anything, but Ellie was pretty sure they'd had a *moment* the other day, when they met up for dinner alone to discuss the counselling job between themselves, and she was aware that she was watching him intently without making her presence known. He was in the process of changing his shirt, throwing aside his light blue v-neck and pulling on a yellow camp counsellor shirt. The older blonde man with the scruffy goatee she didn't recognise; that must have been Billy, was handing them out to all of the gathered group. Sarah and Helen were already wearing theirs, arms around each other, and Natalie had tied her's around her waist. Danny finished putting his own on, but put his battered old denim jacket back over the top once he was done. He never went anywhere without that thing, Ellie had observed. He kept his wallet, keys and phone inside and hated to be seperated from any of them.

'You gonna keep staring or say hello?' Melissa griped from beside Ellie. She had almost completely forgotten the blonde, having forged ahead after Melissa kept losing her fancy sandals in the mud. Clearly she hadn't been as far behind as Ellie thought.

Melissa's voice was enough to get the attention of the others, who all turned to face her.

'Oh, so you decided to show up then?' Natalie called out with a mischievous grin. 'Thought you two had bottled it.' Ellie had no idea where Natalie had picked up the phrase "bottled". Must have been too many British TV shows, she figured. She exchanged a shy smile with Danny, who seemed to return it, looking away.

'We got stuck in the mud.' Melissa said, her voice annoyed.

'Oh, I see, when she's driving, it's *her* car, but when she gets in trouble, suddenly it's "we".' Ellie pointed out with amusement. 'Don't look at me, I had nothing to do with it.'

'You could have pushed harder.' Melissa pouted, before she spotted Billy, marching over to him. 'Anyway, this is your fault! My sandals are ruined and my car's stuck! You better sort it out!' Ellie quickly stepped forward, putting herself between Melissa and Billy. Melissa was still a friend, but, well, she didn't exactly make a great first impression.

'Sorry, I'm Ellie, this is Melissa. You're Billy, right?' she offered diplomatically.

'That's right. And I'm sorry about your car. We'll go down and tow it out later. Get any bags you left in there too. We'll probably have to leave it back by the main road though, rather than tow it all the way here.'

'That's... *fine.*' Melissa said, folding her arms in a sulk, and giving the impression that she was very much *not* "fine".

'Forget the car for a second, did you guys *see* that thing on the way here?' Ellie asked, waving an overly-excited hand to quieten Melissa. The others all turned, giving her sceptical looks. 'The sign?' she asked.

'The old retro thing? I thought it was kinda neat.' Helen spoke up with a smile. She had always liked older things. Ellie bet that floral patterned dress sticking out from under her camp counsellor shirt was vintage.

'Don't worry. We'll be replacing it with something more modern.' Billy said authoritatively, giving a slight smile.

'No, not... Well, yes the sign, but somebody's killed an animal! Dumped it right on there!' Ellie said frantically. A crackle ran like electricity among the group, as they all exchanged looks, some showed surprise, some showed contempt or disbelief.

'I said I heard something!' Sarah said anxiously. 'Like a howl and a yelp!'

'C'mon, it's *Ellie*. It's probably a Halloween store prop from one of those movies she likes.' Natalie said dismissively.

'Hey, it's real, believe me!' Melissa scoffed.

'Yeah, 'cause *Melissa* always tells the truth.' Natalie mocked with her usual grin.

'Look, just come and take a look!' Ellie realised she was sounding frantic. 'It looked like a wolf or coyote or something. It was too mangled to get a good look!'

'There are no wolves around here. Coyotes… maybe, but I don't see how it could end up on *top* of the sign…' Billy frowned, his voice trailing off. 'But whatever it is, we better get it cleaned up ASAP. The owners of the camp are scheduled to stop by one day this week, and we can't have them arriving and seeing that. Danny?' Billy turned to Danny, and gestured for him to follow. 'Come and give me a hand. Melissa, we'll go rescue your car afterwards, so you can come too. Helen, Sarah, show Ellie where she'll be staying.' Billy instructed, and was moving before anybody could protest. Natalie gave him a small, joking wave as he left. Danny had to physically take Melissa's hand and drag her, amongst her protests of having to go anywhere near the corpse. Ellie turned back to the group as Helen and Sarah approached.

'C'mon. Follow me, Ellie. We'll find you one of those camp counsellor shirts too.' Sarah said as she gestured for Ellie to follow.

'Yeah, Herr Kapitan Billy is insisting we wear them in case the owners show up.' Helen joked as she walked beside Helen. 'Although, I kinda like 'em. They're very retro.' She gave a twirl in her shirt. 'What do you think Ellie?' Ellie paused uneasily.

'I think they look very Camp Crystal Lake. And given what I just saw, I'm not convinced that's a good thing...' She answered, voice trailing off with an uneasy glance back in the direction of the sign.

Ellie had to be honest; she felt uneasy about how long they were gone. There was plenty to do around the campsite, beginning with constructing her own bed. Flat packed wooden cots had arrived en masse, doubtlessly for the children's cabins as well as their own, and it seemed to begin with, each of them had to build their own bed. Ellie, now clad in her yellow camp counsellor shirt, figured it was good practice to get used to the task that lay ahead of them, but it was slightly trickier than she had expected. The packaged instructions seemed to consist purely of seperate images of all the parts that came with the bed, and then arrows pointing at them all going together, and then another image of the completed bed. Ellie was no DIY expert, but she could have figured that part out on her own. As she sat on the floor, surrounded by screws and discarded pieces of wooden frame, she wished that Danny would hurry up and get back soon to help lend a hand.

To her surprise, however, it wasn't Danny, but Natalie who opened the cabin, smiling as she walked in. She was wearing a white paper set of coveralls that were already covered in paint. Obviously the others had started on painting one of the cabins.

'Pain in the ass, aren't they? The trick is that although they *look* the same, the head and foot of the bed are actually different parts, with different sized screw fittings. Here.' Natalie came over and sat on the floor next to Ellie, starting to sort the odd arrangement of screws that were now scattered across the wooden panelling of the floor. The cabin that the counsellors were staying in was the one with the recently repaired roof, and Ellie couldn't decide if that was a good or bad thing. She supposed it meant they had the sturdiest ceiling in case of rain, but at the same time, it meant this cabin had probably been the most damaged.

'Thanks.' Ellie smiled in gratitude for the help. Nat just waved a hand, to say to think nothing of it.

'Wasn't sure you'd make it here without strangling Melissa.' Natalie joked as she began to assemble the foot of the bed.

'That makes two of us.' Ellie shot back with a smirk. The two laughed a little. 'Nah, she's okay really, she's just a bit...'

'Melissa?' Natalie finished for her. There was no other word really to describe their blonde friend.

'Yeah, that.' Ellie giggled a little. She paused when she felt something on her neck. A wisp of cold air seemed to blow into the cabin. She looked over at the door. It was shut. Natalie was still focused on attaching one of the legs to the foot of the bed, turning the screw, and hadn't noticed. Her dark hair fell down around her face, and Ellie couldn't even see her features. 'Did you feel that?' Ellie asked quietly. Natalie looked up, and gave a curious shrug.

'Feel what?'

'Some kind of breeze.' Ellie answered, getting up and looking around the cabin.

'Well, you seen the state of this place? Must be a gap in the panels somewhere.' Natalie said dismissively.

'Yeah, but I thought Billy had contractors in to fix up the cabins.' Ellie pointed out, as she moved curiously, hands held out, as if trying to sense the breeze. A moment later, and she felt it again. Her eyes whirled to where it was coming from, and she approached the wall. Hanging on the wall was a picture, with the new logo of the camp proudly emblazoned upon it. It consisted of a rainbow rising over some clip art tents. Ellie somehow doubted that Billy had done much design work on that. In fact, she doubted he had the license to use the image at all, but she figured he hadn't concerned himself about such things.

Curiosity got the better of her, and she lifted the picture off the wall. She almost dropped it when she saw what was lurking behind.

There was a gash through the wood, almost the diameter of the picture. It was a clear cut that had been opened, and had a dark brown stain around it, which reminded Ellie of dried, old blood. She could see the trees outside through it, and feel the gentle breeze coming in. Natalie, having heard her start, came up beside her to look.

'Wow, Billy must have hired some real cow-boys if they missed *that*.' she quipped as she looked at it. Ellie, however, felt a little on edge. Between this and the animal corpse, she was unnerved.

'But what did that? Look at it. The wooden panels on these cabins are a good few inches thick, and it looks like something sliced through the wall like butter. That's not natural decay; something cut through the wall. You can see the splinters.' The splinters in question were old and decaying, but still present. The longer she looked at it, the more certain she was that the staining was dried blood. The odd thing was that it didn't look like somebody had *sawn* through the wood, it had that broken, damaged look around the edge, like one forceful blow had done that.

'Must be some kind of damage from when the camp shut down. I mean, you're right, the panels are so thick, the contractors probably didn't think they'd need replacing. So they just hid it behind a picture.' Natalie shrugged. 'Maybe a deer caught the wall with its antler or something?'

'I can think of at least five reasons that's not possible.' Ellie countered back, but she allowed her-self a smile. Whatever it was, it clearly wasn't an issue anymore. This damage was *old*, and besides, they wouldn't have reopened the camp if there were dangerous wild animals around. She hung the pic-ture back up on the wall, trying to shrug off her uneasiness. 'We better see if there's some spare wood to nail over it though, otherwise it could get cold in the night.' Ellie suggested, trying to take on a more practical role. Before Natalie could reply however, they heard the sound of a jeep pulling up, and the beeping of a horn to signal that the others had returned.

Ellie and Natalie exited the cabin. Ellie was glad of an excuse to stop working on the bed and she suspected Natalie was too. Danny jumped down from the driver's seat and made his way to the rear, where he began to help Melissa with the first of her many designer suitcases piled in the back. Billy, meanwhile, climbed out on the far side, but walked over to meet Ellie. She realised that she was almost rushing over to meet him.

'Did you see it? The animal?' she asked quickly, only then realising how much it had been playing on her mind. Billy gave a shrug.

'No animal there when we got there. The sign was still covered in dried blood though.' His answer did little to calm Ellie's nerves.

'It was *gone*?' she asked, a lump suddenly appearing and tightening in her throat. Billy paused. Ellie wondered if he was considering calling her a liar, to tell her that it had never been there, but he seemed to think better of it.

'You girls must have been real lucky. Way I figure it, whatever put that thing up there must have still been nearby. Must have come back for it shortly after you left.' Billy answered instead, with a cautious glance at Melissa. Ellie wondered if he'd already tried accusing Melissa of making it up. That wouldn't have ended well. There wasn't a teenager alive who could give a bratty meltdown like Melissa when she wanted to.

'Right.' Ellie said uneasily, unable to find other words. Her eyes wandered back to the treeline behind Billy. She felt queasy. 'Are you sure-'

'Look. Whatever it was, it's long gone now.' he cut her off, and Ellie knew that he was just trying to put her mind at rest. 'Must have been a bear. Don't worry though, doubt it'll approach the camp. Too much commotion and movement for it. If it does, just remember what it says in the guidebook.'

'Right. Yeah.' Unlike Melissa, Ellie had actually read the guidebook, but she was now struggling to remember the advice on bears. She was beginning to think this entire trip had been a bad idea. That creeping feeling, that being camp counsellors over the summer was a *mistake*, had been one she'd dismissed as ridiculously comical. She was a horror film fan, she had watched all the *Friday the 13th* films dozens of times (yes, even *Jason Goes to Hell),* she was just being a dumb, silly, fangirl to think that anything *actually* happened to camp counsellors. Hell, how many people must have done this job across America? And how many of *them* got killed by crazed psychopaths? She just had an overactive imagination.

Still, she had no idea what could have put that gash in the wall. Or moved the corpse of the animal. She remembered stopping in the gas station on the way to the camp, and the crazy warnings from the old man working there. That thought lingered, and she swallowed uneasily, before she forcefully shook it off with an actual physical shake of her head, and began to make her way back into the cabin, to continue working on the bed.

Fortunately, the rest of the day passed largely without incident. As long as you counted "without incident" as not counting the blazing argument between Helen and Melissa when Melissa promptly sat back and let everybody else build her bed for her, or the near heart attack Billy had suffered when Natalie had painted a gigantic penis on the side of the community centre while they were working on it. Of course it was quickly covered up, but that didn't stop the insane panic at the possibility of the elusive owners stopping by and seeing it. Ellie was pleased with their paint work so far, however. It was surprising what a difference it made to the camp, and she was thrilled that they had agreed with her suggestion to use brighter, child friendly colours than the usual rustic aesthetic you found at summer camps. While Natalie, Ellie and Danny had worked on painting the community centre a nice sky blue, Helen, Sarah and Melissa had all made a start on one of the cabins each, each in a pastel, friendly shade. Unsurprisingly, Melissa's cabin was still almost entirely a shade of grimy brown. She had barely lifted a finger. The sun had come out and she had decided instead to sunbathe, insisting that they had "ages" anyway.

Ellie thought that a week was not "ages" to prepare the entire camp, but she was officially Melissa'd out at that point, and decided not to say anything.

Soon enough though, they started losing the light, and Billy suggested calling an end to the day's work. He proudly thanked everyone, even Melissa, which Ellie thought showed more grace than she would have in that situation, and then suggested they go about building a campfire. This was definitely a good idea in Ellie's book, not only because campfires and roasting marshmallows was a big part of the experience she was looking forward to, but the truth was, they were all a bunch of city kids, and none of them were super experienced campers, except maybe Danny. Everything they learned during the week prior to the kids arriving would be invaluable to pass on to them during the actual camp course itself. Thinking about it, they were definitely an odd bunch to hire. It was something that piqued Ellie's curiosity now that she thought about it as she made her way back towards the campsite, arms straining with the weight of gathered sticks.

'No, no, no, those are no good.' Billy waved his hands coming over. 'See the moss growing on them? They're too damp. They'll never catch alight.' Ellie paused, sighing, dropping the sticks. She was at least a bit relieved that she didn't have to carry them any further. 'You need dry wood. Look for stuff without soil or moss.' Billy's voice sounded like it was trying to be cheerful, despite obvious annoyance at how much he had to teach this bunch of city kids.

'Sorry. First time camping.' Ellie blushed a little. She felt foolish, but how was she meant to know? She figured the fire would just dry out the wood anyway. '...Hey, do you mind if I ask... why you hired local? I mean, aren't there like, camp counsellor organisations that could have provided you with proper, trained staff?' Ellie felt better just for vocalising the stray thought.

'Most of the official organisations won't touch this place after it closed down. Figured the best way to dodge too many questions was hire some willing high schoolers. Besides, getting to teach you lot how to take care of yourselves out here is half the fun.' he grinned playfully, before giving Ellie a friendly tap on the arm. 'Now c'mon, get back to work. Remember, *dry* wood only.' Ellie found herself giving him an ashamed smile, and turning to get back to work. In retrospect, his comment about nobody wanting to come near the camp should have rung alarm bells, but Ellie was too ashamed by her lack of camping knowledge, and of course, too inexperienced at that point, to pick up on it.

By the time the sun had fully set and the moon hung high in the sky, bright and full, with only a few wispy clouds passing in front of it, the fire was roaring. Ellie huddled close for warmth. She hadn't expected it to get so *cold* at night out in the forest, and had the sleeves of her hoodie pulled down over her hands to keep them warm. Helen and Sarah were snuggled together, each roasting a marshmallow each. Ellie looked over at Danny, who was still in his camp counsellor shirt and denim jacket, and fought the urge to move closer to him. It would be too obvious of a move. She didn't want to seem desperate, and he hadn't approached her, although she *had* thought he had looked at her longingly for a moment. Melissa looked ridiculous, in a big white puffer coat with fur trim, but at least she must have been warm, while Natalie wore a hoodie detailed like a panda, complete with tiny bear ears on the hood.

'So, remember, no food fights, change often, food odours cling to clothing, and if you're a girl, don't wear perfume.' Billy was lecturing them on the best way to avoid attracting bear attention. He gave a pointed look at Melissa at that last one, who just gave him a little sneer from under her big furry hood. Ellie guessed he figured she was the most likely candidate to break that rule. That meant either he was oblivious to Ellie's attempts to get Danny's attention, or she had been so clumsily terrible at it nobody could tell at all. She wasn't sure which was worse. She was pretty sure Natalie had been eyeing up Billy himself too, and Sarah and Helen obviously had each other. She wouldn't be surprised if Melissa was the only single person at the end of the camp. Ellie smiled a little at that thought. Maybe she was being optimistic for herself and Danny, but either way, she felt like it was a big middle finger to every bad eighties horror flick she'd ever seen that the one rich pretty blonde girl was going to be the one who ended up *without* a partner.

'And remember, don't go wandering too far from the camp. This place is called a *marsh* for a reason.' he added with parental tones.

'The marsh is probably the least of your concerns with this place.' Danny said after a moment, and he was fidgeting. Ellie knew that look. It meant that he had something to talk about. Something he'd been keeping in for a while. 'Anybody for a campfire story?' he asked with a massive grin, in what Ellie was sure was his spookiest voice.

'Oh god, like a ghost story? Yawn!' Melissa exclaimed dramatically, actually *saying* the word "yawn" even as she gestured.

'Yeah, except this one is completely true.' Danny smiled.

'Hey, c'mon, you can't tell them that one.' Billy said quickly. 'It'll totally freak everybody out.'

'Oh, now I've *gotta* hear it.' Natalie put in, excitedly leaning in to get closer. Billy glanced at Danny, and then gave a mischievous smile of his own. It seemed that Billy wasn't without a little playfulness of his own.

'You sure? It's not for the faint of heart.' he teased lightly.

'Yeah! Melissa won't believe it, Ellie's into that stuff, and Helen and Sarah will just snuggle if they get scared.' Natalie confirmed, and Ellie felt a little called out.

'Hey, I like horror *movies*. Doesn't mean I wanna hear some ghost story at some creepy camp.' Ellie said defensively.

'Well, it won't be creepy once we're done working on it, and don't pretend you can walk away now without knowing. I know you.' Danny teased her, moving in slightly. Ellie gave him a coy smile. Okay, maybe there was a good reason to hear this out.

'Alright then. Try and terrify me. But I warn you, I saw *Halloween* when I was eight years old.' Ellie challenged, teasing him right back. Technically it had been *Halloween IV: The Return of Michael Myers* and her mom had been *livid* when she found out, but those kinds of details seemed unnecessary here.

'Okay then. Let me tell you the story of the Mirror Monster.' Danny grinned again. Melissa scoffed and rolled her eyes.

'The "Mirror Monster"? C'mon, can't you do better than that?' she asked, removing one of her impressively fluffy mittens to examine her manicured fingernails. Ellie was certain she had only done that for effect.

'I didn't name him. But that's what they call him. To understand though, you have to go back. All the way back to the summer of 1979...' Danny smiled wistfully as he looked into the flames, and for a moment Ellie wondered if he was expecting a flashback to begin, like they were in the movies. Instead, all they were met by were the dancing orange flames. Ellie could feel the intense heat on her face, almost burning her cheeks, and yet the rest of her body still shivered with the cold. 'Nobody knows the boy's name, not anymore, but they know the story.

He was born with extreme deformities. Really bad stuff. Enough that he grew up too scared to see the other kids. He was afraid they'd make fun of him, tease him, bully him. He stayed indoors all the time. He was even home educated. But one summer, a youth worker suggested it might do him some good to come and work at the camp. Get out into the fresh air, be with other teenagers his age. That youth worker had faith in humanity. It was misplaced.' Danny paused, only for dramatic effect, looking each of the campers in their eyes. Only Melissa didn't look back, still focused on her nails. 'As soon as the teenagers saw him, they started to mock him. Teasing names. Taunting jeers. They tore at his self esteem. Until he'd snapped. He'd tried to fight back. He got angry and lashed out, and the group of teens teamed together and beat him. Somehow in the scuffle, he'd been lost to the marsh. Sunk beneath the muddy water. The other teenagers didn't mention it. They covered it up. They wanted to hide what they did.'

'And his body rests out here somewhere? Ohhh, spooky.' Melissa rolled her eyes.

'No, he obviously came back for revenge, right?' Ellie cut in. She knew how these stories went. The tragic origin of the killer was just the start.

'Oh yes.' Danny's eyes flashed in the orange light of the fire. 'He crawled out of the marsh that very night, face swollen and beaten. He looked more monstrous than ever. He stalked through the night, and his first kill was the vain, rich, blonde counsellor.' he paused only to look at Melissa. 'Remind

25

you of anyone?'

'I'm not vain. It's not vanity if you're *actually* pretty.' Melissa shot back, causing a snigger from Natalie.

'This girl was busy doing her hair in the mirror, hoping to seduce one of the boys there. He approached behind her, and smashed her face right through it.' Danny continued, ignoring Melissa's dramatics. 'He killed her stone dead, but when he saw his reflection, he was horrified! He took a shard of the mirror and an old camping rope, and tied it around his face. He swore nobody would ever see his visage again. Only what was reflected *outwards*.'

'Hang on, if he had a mirror tied to his face, how did he see?' Sarah asked sceptically. Danny went to reply, opened his mouth, and closed it again after a few moments.

'Huh. Never thought of that.' Danny muttered. Ellie, however, was now interested.

'Hey, don't stop. I'm getting into this!' she said with excitement.

'See, told you, into it.' Natalie mocked. Ellie just waved a hand to make her be quiet, so that Danny could continue.

'Well, after that he slaughtered the other campers. When the first of the kids showed up there, they found a massacre. After that, they shut the camp down. But they said the Mirror Monster was always out there… lurking.' Danny finished.

'Great story. Creepy kid monster in the woods. Nice.' Melissa said dismissively.

'Oh, that's just the *start*. Because, see, six years ago, they tried to reopen the camp. They rebuilt all the cabins. *These* cabins.' Danny gestured to the cabins all around them. 'They got ready to reopen. But a week before opening, something happened. Somebody attacked the campers there. One girl survived. But she swore it was him. The *Mirror Monster*. She thought she had killed him. She said she drove an axe right through his skull and left him in the swamp, but when the police came, they couldn't find a body...' Ellie felt a sudden chill, and she thought back to the damage to the hut wall. What if that had been this killer? What if it wasn't just creepy *looking*, but the actual leftover from a murder scene? The brown stain on the wood, the one that had looked so much like old blood, flashed across her eyes. She closed them and tried to force the image from her mind. 'After that, every year, some mystery killing happened. Sometimes it was hikers. One time a group of hunters. The authorities blamed bear attacks, of course. One family had an old lodge out this way. They were the ones who solved the mystery. They said it was definitely the Mirror Monster. They'd seen him invade their home. Same grotty mirror, same deformed flesh. Only their daughter survived. She ended it when she shot him. This time, he really *was* dead. The police took his corpse to the morgue, and made the best identification he could. He had the same physical deformities as the boy from '79, he was the right age, but the boy's mother had long since disappeared. The theory was that he had survived the attack and grown up out here, in the wild, all alone, more animal now than man.'

'But he's dead now, right?' Helen asked uneasily. Sarah rubbed her knee and snuggled a little closer to her to keep her comforted.

'That's where the story gets *really* crazy. See, somebody funded the burial of the body. Nobody knows who. Some theorised it was his long lost father. Others, that it might have been some rich sponsor who felt sympathy for the boy he had been. Who knows? But anyway, they buried him at a graveyard, not far from the marshlands.' Danny went on, and Ellie noticed that by now even Melissa had stopped joking and interfering with the story. 'But a year later, all that was there was a muddy hole. Now, some people think somebody dug him up for a prank, but others, they said, if you looked closely at the hole, the dirt hadn't been dug *up.* It had been pushed *out.* Like somebody had dug their way out... Like something had *come back from the dead.*'

'Okay, but that has to be a load of bull, right?' Natalie laughed. 'I mean, you had me going for a moment, but what, he was a zombie now?' she asked sceptically.

'Hey, look, these are *facts*. You can look it up. The murders. The missing. It all happened. I'm not saying a zombie came back, but... Well, somehow the body wasn't in his grave anymore... And sure enough, people started disappearing again.' Danny continued.

'Honestly, this bit is true. The whole urban

legend of the Mirror Monster is why they never re-opened the camp.' Billy input. 'But obviously, there was no *zombie* stalking people out here. Hikers get lost all the time and bears *are* a real problem out here.'

'That was, until last year.' Danny took over smoothly. 'A group of friends went camping out this way. Somebody or something attacked them. There was one survivor. She described the stink of rotting flesh, pale mottled skin, and on their attacker's face? A *mirror*.' Danny took time to smirk. 'Anyway, she somehow managed to chain him to a boulder and throw it into the marsh, dragging him down into the depths for the rest of time.'

'Oh *come on*!' Elle laughed, leaning back and clapping her hands together. Silence followed as the others looked at her. 'That's just the ending of *Jason Lives*!' She exclaimed. This was followed by more silence. 'You know, *Friday the 13th: Part VI*? With the Alice Cooper song?' Ellie was only greeted by more blank faces. 'Tommy Jarvis chains Jason to a boulder and leaves him at the bottom of Crystal Lake?' she asked again, but still only more blank faces greeted her. 'Come on! It's a great movie!' Nobody replied for a moment.

'Hey, I'm just telling you what the survivor said.' Danny laughed, throwing his hands up defensively.

'Actually, that part of the story is at least *kind* of true as well.' Billy joined in again. 'There were killings of the campers, and they did send the killer to the bottom of the marsh. It's why I finally got approval to reopen this place. As far as the locals are concerned, the killer's gone.'

'Of course, that meant the killer's body was never recovered, so they could never verify the "zombie" story. Could have just been a guy using the old local legend, wearing a rubber mask. Like a really messed up *Scooby Doo* episode.' Danny confessed, and then he paused, before lowering his voice a little. 'Or, maybe it really was the Mirror Monster. Maybe he really can't die? And maybe, just *maybe*, he's still out there, lurking at the bottom of that marsh, waiting for a group foolhardy enough to return to his swamp...' Danny grinned.

'Get outta mah swamp!' Natalie suddenly yelled in a thick, fake accent. Was it Welsh? Or Irish? Ellie had no idea, but she was pretty sure she was trying to do a terrible Shrek impression. Either way, it made her flinch, and Melissa almost fell off the small log she was sat on, which caused Natalie to howl with laughter. Even Danny looked shocked.

'Dammit, you nearly made me wet myself!' Helen giggled, glaring at Natalie.

'Sorry, too perfect, couldn't pass it up.' Natalie held her hands up defensively. After that, the night soon fell into giggles, but Ellie couldn't shake the memory of that story, the strange gash in the cabin, or the mysteriously slain animal...

Morning came, and Ellie had to admit that the hastily constructed bed was pretty comfortable. She had been ready to rough it out in the sticks, but actually it was probably better quality than her bed back home. The air was chilly and damp, though, and Ellie didn't really want to leave her cheap sleeping bag. It was old, and still smelled a little musty from where it had been in storage. Apparently, it had been her mom's when she had been younger. She hadn't been able to afford a new one. She yawned, and began to stretch. She was aware that footsteps had awoken her. The cabin was the one set aside for the girls, and she looked to see Natalie on her way out. She looked for Helen and Sarah, both of whom had already left. Ellie must have slept through that. Opposite her, Melissa was still sound asleep in a fancy baby pink sleeping bag. Ellie decided not to bother her, and instead slipped out of bed. She picked up her bundled towel and toiletries, all arranged last night along with her clothes for the day and made her way out into the fresh dawn air, quickly slipping her sneakers on as she did so.

She was only wearing a vest top and baggy pajama shorts, but she didn't care if the others saw her like this. They'd been friends for years, and she was well beyond the pride of appearance. Okay, except maybe for Danny. She'd want to get dressed before he saw her, but she had to make her way to the shower block before that could happen anyway. She made her way down, the brisk morning air being enough to fully wake her before she even got to the showers. The shower block was, at least, new looking. The brick work looked fresh and the electric generator hooked up to the side, doubtlessly to provide electric heated showers, was definitely brand new. It must have cost a fair bit to construct, Ellie realised, and not for the first time she wondered about Billy's financial situation, to revitalise the camp so completely. Either way, she was happy to enjoy the warm shower, and it was impressively warm, despite the electric heat, and was busy drying herself off and getting dressed when she heard the cry from outside.

'God *dammit*! You have to be *KIDDING* me!' Danny's voice cut through the air. It was full of disbelief and fury, and Ellie had only heard him sound that angry once before; and that was when some careless student had put a dent in his brand new SUV and driven off, leaving Danny to discover the damage later on. Ellie had been there then, and never heard him so angry.

She hurried out of the shower block, quickly wrapping a towel around her still damp hair. She had at least managed to get changed into the rest of her clothes, although she was practically hopping as she hit the ground to get her other sneaker on in time. She hurried over to see that, just as before, the source of Danny's ire was the state of his precious vehicle, although from this distance Ellie couldn't see what was wrong with it. The others, minus Melissa who was probably still sleeping through all of this, had gathered as well.

Danny let off a string of expletives as Ellie got by his side, and she lightly touched his shoulder.

'What? What is it?' she asked, concerned, unsure of what could have made Danny so furious.

'*Look*!' Danny gestured angrily to the tires. Ellie looked down, and it took her a moment to process what she was seeing.

They had been slashed. All four of them.

'Mine's the same, man.' Billy emerged from around the side of his own jeep, looking frustrated, but a great deal calmer than Danny. 'All four tires, flat.'

'This wasn't a goddamn bear!' Danny said furiously.

'Maybe it was the Mirror Monster.' Natalie suggested with a big grin.

'*Not* funny Nat! Some little asshole's done this to my car! It's going to cost a *fortune* for four new tires!' Danny stressed. 'And how the hell are we gonna get back to town from out here!?' he added, gesturing wildly to Billy to indicate both their cars were now out of action.

'Where did you leave Melissa's car, once you towed it out of the mud yesterday?' Ellie asked, taking a wild guess the sporty convertible might now be their only hope.

'Took it back onto the main road and left it parked on the side there.' Billy answered. 'It's a bit of a walk, but we could do it. Walk back there, then there's a garage in town.' he suggested thoughtfully, before nodding to himself as if he had already made a decision. 'Yeah, let's do that.'

'Uh, aren't you concerned about who *did* this?'

Sarah asked cautiously.

'Probably just some punk kids. When I first came here, I found some old beer cans in one of the cabins. I reckon kids come out here sometimes to drink, smoke weed, that kind of thing. Probably didn't know it was back in action and thought they'd cause some trouble.' Billy said with a dismissive shake of his head.

'I dunno about you, but I wanna catch 'em. Get their parents to pay for my new tires!' Danny growled.

'They could be anywhere by now. It's a big area. Besides, we're better off focusing on fixing the problem than chasing after who's to blame.' Billy said diplomatically. 'We also need to get to work on the camp. We can't let this set us back. We've only got four days until opening'. Danny took a deep, frustrated breath.

'Okay. Okay. Fine. So, what's the plan?' he asked, and Ellie knew that he was trying to keep himself calm. She considered stepping closer, putting a hand on his arm, but she thought better of it.

'I better stay here. I know where everything is and the work plan.' Billy decided. 'Danny, you know your way around vehicles, right? You and Melissa head back into town. There's a garage there, run by a fella named Gareth. Tell him Billy sent you. He's got a truck, he can come out this way, help us sort out the cars.' Billy instructed. Ellie felt a sudden pang of jealousy at the idea of Danny and Melissa heading into town together, while she was left behind.

'I could go.' she said before she realised she had spoken. Danny looked at her, and she blushed, but he gave her a smile of appreciation. 'I mean, I can help Danny.' she added quickly. Billy, unfortunately, shook his head.

'I've only known Melissa for half a day and I already know she won't let anybody else drive her car. Besides, you're a good worker, and you have great ideas. I'd much rather have you here working than Melissa.' Billy smiled. Ellie knew *exactly* what he was doing, offering her a compliment to make her stay, buttering her up nicely. It was textbook leadership skills when you had to get somebody to do something without causing a problem, but she also had to admit it was working.

'Okay, fine.' Ellie smiled, before looking at Danny. 'Don't be gone too long though, right?' she said with a smile, before her stomach knotted with nerves and she realised she was being a little too forward.

'And stay with Melissa any longer than I need to? Trust me, I'll be back as soon as I can.' Danny laughed slightly, and Ellie giggled too.

'Right then. Guess we'd better wake the princess up, and get to work.' Billy nodded, plan decided. Natalie grinned.

'Ohhh, let me do it!' she smiled, and ran off towards the cabin. Ellie just rolled her eyes. She had no idea what prank Natalie was planning but she was sure it would be an amusing way to wake Melissa up.

Ellie's ears were still ringing from Melissa's screams several hours later, as she continued to paint the community centre. She didn't know where Natalie had gotten the rubberised, moving snake from, but it had been pretty convincing when she'd shown Ellie afterwards, and had definitely been enough to wake Melissa and get her out of bed *quickly.* Luckily, Melissa calmed down once she understood the seriousness of the current situation. Either that, or she was just happy to get away from Natalie and the camp for a bit, but she left with Danny promptly, which was impressive for Melissa, who Ellie didn't think had ever successfully gotten ready in under an hour in her life before.

Luckily, she was finding the painting peaceful. Billy had taken over painting around the big propane gas tank mounted to the side of the centre, and left Ellie to paint the window frames. This was a much more delicate process than it sounded, as the glass was already mounted, but Ellie was enjoying the fiddly detail. She had managed to persuade Billy to let her paint them yellow, adding to the summery look of the now mostly sky blue cabin. Unfortunately, with Danny gone, and the remaining girls all surprisingly height deficient between them, they had needed a ladder to get to the roof, where Natalie was currently propped. She seemed to be balanced precariously as she stuffed something into the back pocket of her jeans. Ellie was happy that she didn't have to go up there, because she didn't like how stable that ladder looked. Helen and Sarah were supposed to be working on one of the dormitory cabins, but Ellie hadn't seen them in a while, and assumed that they had snuck away for a quick make-out session somewhere in the woods.

There was still a gnawing sense of doubt in the pit of Ellie's stomach. Nothing about this place felt right. The strange animal, the slashed tires, the damaged wall, the ghost story from the night before, it all felt like... well, Ellie knew exactly what it felt like. A cheesy horror movie. But they weren't *real*, right? She was being silly. It was summer, it was a camp, she was with her friends. She should have just sat back and enjoyed herself. The focus on painting was at least taking her mind off of everything quite effectively. In fact, she was feeling relaxed, her mind focused only on the falling of her brush strokes and the smell of fresh paint, until the ear splitting screech of terror broke her from her trance. She turned so quickly she left a streak of yellow paint right across the otherwise perfect blue finish of the wall, but that instantly became the least of her concerns, because she saw Helen running out of the woods, at full sprint.

Her vintage glasses frame was skewered on her face, her auburn hair messy, and her camp counsellor shirt was hanging loosely off the shoulders of her vintage dress. Ellie prayed the red mark on the shirt was paint, but as she closed the distance between her and Helen, she saw that it could only be the *other thing*. Too wet, too shiny, too *sticky* for paint. Blood. A huge gash of blood, right along Helen's shoulder.

'What is it!? What happened!?' Ellie cried, grabbing Helen by the shoulders. Helen threw herself into Ellie's arms, and Ellie had no choice but to embrace her in a hug. Natalie was already making her way down the ladder in concern, and Billy was running over in a hurry.

'It was him! The Mirror Monster! He's *real*!' Helen sobbed furiously. Ellie pulled back, lifting Helen up to look into her eyes.

'What? What do you mean?' Ellie asked. Natalie half fell off the ladder as she jumped down to run over.

'You're kidding, right? This is a really bad joke!' Natalie said desperately, but anybody could know from looking at Helen this was no simple prank. The blood on her shirt was *real*, as were the tears in her eyes. Ellie's eyes were drawn to the gash in her clothes, and she could see the angry cut below, looking sore and tender. Definitely not fake. Suddenly, Ellie felt her blood run cold as she realised something else.

'Wait. Helen, where's Sarah?' she asked, her voice edged with fear. Helen just looked at Ellie, sobbed, and slowly shook her head. As if Sarah was gone. Sarky Sarah. Who had been Ellie's friend since her first day at high school. *Gone.* 'No...' Ellie found herself saying.

'Show us.' Natalie said quickly. Helen shook her head in fear. 'You have to show us. We need to know what happened.'

'He killed her, alright? He came out of no-where with this... this... curved... blade thing, and he drove it right through the back of her head while we were-' Helen paused to sniffle. '-while we were...' she trailed off. Ellie didn't need Helen to say what they had been doing. She knew.

'Who? Who could do that?' Natalie asked, her voice sounding dry.

'She said it was the Mirror Monster...' Ellie pointed out.

'Dammit Ellie! This isn't one of your horror movies! Sarah is-' Natalie stopped, choking on her own sorrow. Ellie was aware that she was crying too, and she didn't know if it was because she was beginning to process the loss of Sarah, or whether she was stung by Natalie's words. The three of them stood for a moment, their grief bitter and raw. And then slowly, the three of them hugged each other, holding each other through the tears.

A moment passed. A simple beat. And then something twigged in Ellie's mind. Three of them. It never felt right when there were only three of them. They were a group. A team. A club. Call them what you wanted, it was always her, Sarah, Helen, Melissa, Natalie and Danny, but right now something else felt amiss.

'Billy!' Ellie suddenly exclaimed. He wasn't part of their group, so of course in the trauma she hadn't thought of him, but now she suddenly real-ised he was missing. 'Where's Billy!?' Silence suddenly passed among the trio as their eyes scanned all around. Ellie tried to think through the fog and the horror of what had just happened. Where had Billy been before it had started?

The gas tank! That was right! He had been painting around the gas tank.

Without a moment's hesitation, Ellie took off in the direction of where she had last seen their leader. Footsteps told her Natalie and Helen were following, but she didn't look behind her. She skidded around the edge of the community hut, her sneakers sliding on the ground, but Billy was nowhere to be seen. Her eyes dropped to the ground, where she could see a discarded paint brush laying on the ground, and noticed a pool of blue paint from where a paint can had been kicked over. As if there had been a struggle.

'Did it get Billy?' Natalie asked quickly.

'No blood.' Ellie said, her voice just as rapid.

'M-maybe it dragged him off?' Natalie suggested uneasily.

'W-why would it do that? Why kill Sarah but drag Billy away!?' Sarah sobbed.

'I don't know! You're the horror expert, Ellie!' Natalie turned to Ellie. Ellie just glared back, wide eyed, confused, desperate, her entire body trembling. She felt sick, somehow warm but ice cold at the same time, queasy, with vomit urging and rumbling in the bottom of her throat. Like she was living in a nightmare. She could barely grasp what was happening.

'T-those are movies! I-I don't know! Maybe he got away? We need to find him! Quickly!' Ellie said after a moment.

'BILLY!?' Sarah called out through a sob.

'No, no, don't shout! You might draw out whatever's out there!' Ellie quickly covered Sarah's mouth.

'We've got to find him, and fast. We'd better split up. We can cover more ground that way.' Natalie decided. Ellie paused, and just gave her a long, hard, look. Natalie froze, and looked back at her. 'Yeah, okay, even *I* know that was a dumb thing to say.' she admitted after a moment. Any levity between the two was lost however the instant Helen sobbed again.

'Sarah… She's gone…' The words were muffled by horrible sobs. Ellie took a deep breath and tried to think. Yes, horror movies were just *movies*. But what horror fan hadn't imagined themselves in this exact scenario? How many times had she watched random teenagers get sliced to pieces on screen, smug in the knowledge that it'd never happen to her? Sitting there looking at the screen, rolling her eyes as Terri went skinny dipping alone in the dead of night, as Pam fell over nothing, as Tina ran up the stairs instead of out the door, as Nancy happily jumped in the car with her should-be dead friends or as Laurie hid in a closet instead of finishing off Michael Myers. She would never make those mistakes, right? At least, that was what she always told herself…

'Okay. We need to stick together. Find some

way to defend ourselves. Get some tools or something.' Ellie said, thinking hard about what she thought would be best to do.

'There's an archery range here, right?' Natalie suggested uneasily.

'Yeah, but do any of us know how to use a bow and arrow?' Ellie asked incredulously. A moment's silence passed. 'That's what I thought. Let's get some tools. Hammers. Maybe a machete.'

'Who actually *has* a machete in their tools?' Natalie asked.

'I don't know! I'm not a ... fixer... tool... girl!' Ellie waved her arms around in hysteria as she tried to think of the right words. 'I just know we need weapons!'

'There's... a shed. I think. Where we got the paint brushes from.' Helen spoke up, her voice quaking and uneasy, but filling with determination. 'There were some tools in there.'

'Right. Shed. Yeah. Let's go.' Ellie said, hoping that she sounded more determined than she felt.

They moved quickly. A little *too* quickly. Ellie almost slipped and fell over a discarded stick. She'd never have forgiven herself if she'd been *that* girl who'd tripped over barely anything. After that, Ellie suggested that they move slowly. They were safer if they moved slowly and kept in control, making sure they covered all angles at one time, so nobody could sneak up on them. When they reached the shed, however, Ellie felt her heart freeze for a second time that afternoon. Or was it evening? They had been working for a long time and the sun was already going down.

It had clearly been ransacked. A toolbox had been overturned and screwdrivers, nails, pliers and other assorted tools Ellie couldn't identify littered the ground. Several large garden implements had been thrown onto the floor. Paint tins had been tipped over. And on the wall, Ellie could see the faded imprint of where a sickle had been hanging.

Helen's words replayed in Ellie's mind. "Curved blade thing". Like a sickle.

'He was here.' Ellie said breathlessly. 'He came here, to the shed, to find a weapon. He was here while we were out there…. *Painting!*' The thought that this monster had been lurking, watching them, arming himself, it made her feel sick all over again. How long had he been observing them? Obviously since the night before, right? To have slashed the tires. Even longer, perhaps. Had he watched them while they slept? Ellie imagined him, toying with the idea of slicing them open unaware, but then deciding instead it would be more fun to chase them while they were awake. She imagined that he liked their fear.

'There must be something here we can use!' Natalie said quickly, scooping down to pick up a discarded hammer. She swung it experimentally. She gave a nod of appreciation. Helen picked up some kind of fire poker, and tested the sharp end with her finger. She pulled it back when it drew blood. That left Ellie. She looked over at the worktop, and spotted a chainsaw, knocked onto its side, under a grimy window. She hesitated.

'Nah, that's stupid.' she said under her breath. A chainsaw? Sure, they used those in horror movies all the time, but they were weighty, noisy, and she had no idea how to use one. She looked for something else, spotting a particularly long screwdriver. She picked it up, and looked at it with disappointment. It would at least hurt if she stabbed somebody with it, she figured. It was better than nothing.

'Should have gone for the bow and arrow.' Natalie said under her breath as she looked at Ellie's puny weapon. Both girls tried to crack a smile, but it failed to come for either of them. Helen seemed to adjust her grip on the poker.

'Okay. I'm ready. I'm going to get him for what he did to Sarah!' she said angrily.

'No! Look, whoever he is, monster or human, he's a killer. We're not! We don't go after him! We just, we need to find Billy, then we need to get the hell out of here!' Ellie exclaimed. 'I mean, what's the one dumb thing nobody ever does in a horror movie?' The others looked to her, but none of them answered. '*Leave*. Just *leave*. Get the hell out of Dodge!' They looked at her blankly in response to that too. Ellie supposed sometimes she forgot the others didn't watch old movies like her. 'Outta town.' She clarified. 'Let's get Billy, and run. It's not that far back to the main road. Danny and Melissa will be coming back that way any time! We find them and we all get out of here and go to the police, before anybody else gets hurt!'

'What about....' Helen swallowed uneasily. 'What about Sarah's body? What about the *thing* that did this?'

'Let the police handle it! We're three scared girls with some garden tools. They've got guns. Once we've found Billy, we've gotta get outta here. It's our only chance!' Ellie said desperately. Natalie seemed to nod.

'I agree. I don't care if he's a zombie or just some psycho in a costume, I don't wanna fight him!' she agreed. Ellie wanted to give Natalie a smile, to show her appreciation that she backed her up, but no smile came to her lips when she tried. Reluctantly, gripping the poker tightly, Helen nodded.

'O-okay. Yeah. Let's go.' Helen marched towards the exit to the shed, poker in hand, pushing past Ellie. Ellie didn't know quite what was happening in her head, but imagined that now she had decided, she just wanted to get out of there. Unfortunately, it was something that would never happen for Helen.

As soon as she went to leave the shed, there was a sudden whistle, and a sickening thud. Something slammed into Helen's skull, piercing it. A blade. Ellie and Natalie both screamed, leaping backwards, crashing into the workbench behind them. Two monstrous, decaying hands reached around, one placed on the blade embedded in Helen's head, and one on the wooden handle of the sickle, and then they viciously turned it, like a crank wheel. It caused Helen's head to spin around with a snap, until her shocked, horrified face, eyes rolled back, was facing directly at Ellie. Her body still faced her killer. And then the hands released her, and her body crumpled to the ground.

Behind her stood something like nothing Ellie had ever seen. She knew now why Helen had been so convinced the killer was really the Mirror Monster. It was because the *thing* that stood before her was definitely not human. Oh, it might have been once, but not anymore. It wore a heavy brown coat, so worn and battered that at points the outside had melted away to look like patches of huge spiderwebs on its surface. Beneath that, there was a black shirt, but torn apart, with sticky, wet looking flesh and bone protruding from the tears. She could see his rib cage, and although she thought she might have imagined it, perhaps a blackened heart beating too. The dark jeans it wore were equally battered and torn, revealing the same mottled brown flesh and a clear shin bone beneath the tear. Its hands were gaunt, but huge, wearing the tatty remains of gloves that barely held together over thick, lumpy digits coated in the same bloated, damp flesh. And then there was its face. Its bald head was visible, its glistening, rotting skin easy to see, wisps of grey hair dangling down its shoulders, but its face... Its face was hidden completely. By a shard of mirror. The mirror was tied onto its face with a battered looking golden rope, that for a moment Ellie thought looked like golden pigtails, or perhaps even a halo around its head. But it was definitely no halo, and the creature was no angel. Its chest rose and fell, even though it didn't seem to be taking a breath at all, and for a moment its head tilted down at Helen's body, as if admiring its handiwork.

Ellie felt her world freeze. She *knew* this moment. The moment where the killer stood before its victims, and they just stared. Those moments where Ellie would be giggling and yelling "run" at the screen but they never did. Now she understood it. Her legs had turned to lead. The thought of moving took so much effort she thought she might collapse. She was rooted to the spot.

Slowly, the Mirror Monster raised its head, staring directly at Ellie. It tilted its head slightly. If Ellie hadn't been so terrified for her life, she'd have appreciated the classic slasher monster gesture. As it was, however, it was the small push she needed to snap right out of her paralysis. With no way out past the creature, they only had one choice.

'The window!' Ellie yelled, grabbing the chainsaw off the workbench and throwing it at the glass. She was surprised by the weight, but in a good way, as the heavy chainsaw sailed and smashed through the dirty glass easily. Ellie quickly sprang up over the workbench and crouched, diving out the window, wincing as she felt glass lash at her. She turned to grab Natalie as she jumped through behind her, pulling Natalie down even as a tearing sound told her Natalie's camp counsellor shirt had snagged on a shard of broken window. She pulled harder and Natalie was free, although a huge chunk of yellow fabric was left behind.

A moment later, a huge, decaying hand claimed it for its own.

Ellie wasn't sure she had ever run this fast or for this long in her life. Natalie was right beside her, but eventually the two had to stop. Ellie's lungs burned and screamed for oxygen, and she was doubled over. She was the movie nerd, not an athlete. She couldn't keep running for much longer. Natalie too seemed to be wheezing, although she suspected that might be because of her smoking habit. She'd kicked it in the last year pretty successfully, but she guessed the ill effects still lingered.

'What do we do!? What the hell do we do!?' Natalie shrieked.

'W-we get out of here! We can't do anything against *that*! W-we just have to hope Billy's okay.' Ellie said quickly, unsure if it was her panic or cowardice talking. Surely running was the best option? Again, in those old horror movies that she loved, the characters always stuck around too long when they should run. Now she was calling it. Time to *run*.

'What about Melissa and Danny? W-we need to warn them before they come back!' Natalie pointed out. Ellie paused. She hadn't thought of that. Because... Oh god, what if it had gotten Melissa and Danny as they walked back to Melissa's car?

'We just need to get to the road out of here. It's

open. It's clear. Once we're on that, we'll be safe.' Ellie wished she believed her words, but somehow they sounded hollow. She began to look around, as did Natalie.

'Great. Great plan.' Natalie gulped nervously. 'Just one question though. Where the heck *are* we?' Ellie realised what Natalie was saying. In their fear they'd bolted into the darkness of the trees, and now they had no idea where they were. There was no obvious way back, and with the fading light it was practically night already. Everywhere looked the same. Any path they took could lead them further away from the camp. They could wander for days out there, lost, before the creature caught them.

'Okay. We just... Uh, we need to think. What way did we come from? We can... We can retrace our steps.' Ellie wasn't sounding confident, and she knew it. She was completely disoriented, and the thought of going back the way they came exactly would just lead them to a confrontation with that... *thing.*

'I'm not going back *there!*' Natalie insisted, and Ellie had to admit, she felt like agreeing.

'We'll never find our way out of here if we don't get back to the camp!' Ellie countered, and Natalie froze, looking behind her uneasily, but seeming to agree.

'Okay. Okay. But how do we find it? We were running... every way. I don't have a clue where we are!' Natalie made a good point, and Ellie had no idea how to answer. She wasn't sure why Natalie was even asking her. Natalie still assumed Ellie was the expert because she liked horror movies, but she was certainly no outdoorsman. She had no idea how to navigate a thick forest. She didn't even know if they were in a forest or a wood. What was the difference? There were a lot of trees. That was all she knew. She was pretty certain, however, now wasn't the time for such thoughts.

'I... I guess we just pick a direction. We start walking. I mean, this place is a marsh, right? So if the ground starts to get boggier, we know we're going the wrong way. We're getting deeper into it. So, then we just turn around. Head back?' Ellie's voice ended in a question, as if she desperately wanted confirmation. Neither herself nor Natalie were ever particularly outdoorsy people, and Ellie had no idea if marshland worked the way she thought, but she doubted Natalie did either.

'Okay. Okay. So, uh, let's try.... This way.' Natalie began to move, walking through the trees. Ellie looked around nervously for pursuit, and then began to follow. She realised she was still clutching the screwdriver uneasily. She looked to see that Natalie was still gripping her hammer. Good. They were still armed. They still had a chance. They just had to get out of there. They had to keep going, before it got too dark. Once they lost the last of the light, Ellie knew they stood no chance. Lost in these woods at night was dangerous *without* an undead killer on the loose, if Billy's stories about bears were to be believed but add to that being pursued by something that Ellie now *knew* to be supernatural, and, well, she knew how much trouble they were in. Just last night she had been startled by how dark the camp had gotten, always having been used to some presence of city light, and now out here, she knew they'd be truly screwed if they let it get to that point. She took one last look behind her and hurried her pace, moving to catch up with Natalie.

Ellie was only a few steps behind when it happened. With a sickening snap and a crunch, something clamped together around Natalie's leg. Natalie didn't even scream, but the blood splatter reached Ellie's face. Slowly, in pure shock, her body trembling, Natalie looked down. Ellie's eyes followed. Metal teeth were clamped around her leg. A bear trap. Ellie had seen them on television, but she had no idea they were *real* things until now. Somehow, her brain told her it should be rusty and old, some ancient trap laid by the rotting monster, but the metal on it was shiny and new, and not just where it was splattered with the crimson blood of Natalie. Without thinking, Ellie quickly rushed around to get in front of Natalie, grabbing her by the shoulders.

'Are... are you alright!?' Ellie knew it was a stupid question as soon as she asked. Natalie was trembling, coated in sweat, and her body buckled as she fell forwards, vomiting. The fall tore at her trapped leg, causing a sickly, wet, squelching tearing noise that Ellie could only assume was flesh. Her hands were on the dirt and one knee was down, but her foot was still embedded in the trap. This time she screamed. 'Ohmigod, Natalie, just... just hang on...' Ellie bent down to look at the trap. The metal teeth were almost touching. They'd cut through the flesh and bone as if her leg was made from paper. Ellie could see Natalie's shin bone jutting from the injured leg. She had to bite back her own vomit. All those horror movies she'd watched, all those great gore effects by Tom Savini, and yet seeing the real thing was so very different. Somehow, knowing it was real triggered some deep down reaction that she didn't even know she possessed, fear and panic and revulsion, and she realised she was almost trembling as much as Natalie. 'J-just, hold on...' Ellie grabbed the teeth, and tried to pry them apart, grunting with effort, but they didn't budge.

'H-hurry!' It was the first word Natalie had spoken since the trap had closed, and even that took effort. Ellie realised she had no idea what the trapped girl was thinking, but her body was trembling even more. She must have been going into shock. Ellie tried to remember what she knew about first aid. They were all meant to take a first aid course as part of the job of being camp counsellors, but it was to be during the week. It was scheduled for Wednesday. And she doubted it covered bear traps.

'Just... just, hold on.' Ellie looked at the screwdriver in her hands. The fallen hammer from Natalie. Maybe she could try and use them to pry the trap apart? She inserted the screwdriver into the trap's teeth, and then knocked it with the hammer, trying to use the extra force to wrench the trap open. All she did however was move it enough for it to then snap back together on Natalie's leg with each jolt, causing Natalie to scream. 'Sorry! Sorry!' Ellie panicked.

'Ellie...' Natalie's voice was weak. 'Please...'

'I'm trying! I don't know what to do!' Ellie practically screamed, sobbing, her hands covered in Natalie's blood. *So* much blood. If she didn't do something soon, Natalie would bleed out. Ellie for a moment rested her head in her hands where she was crouched. God, what could she do? She couldn't leave Natalie. No way. No matter what. But if she didn't do something soon, if she couldn't *think* of something, Natalie would *die.* Another friend would be dead and this time it would be her fault. She let out a desperate sob.

'L-look... The... bastard... didn't want us to escape...' Natalie's voice shook, but she pointed a shaking finger. Ellie's eyes followed, and she saw in the darkness several gleaming objects on the ground. More bear traps. Ellie let out a furious sob and drove an angry fist into the blood soaked earth.

'It was a trap. He must have... He placed them all around. A perimeter so we couldn't escape!' Ellie's voice trembled with anger and frustration. There was no way past them all. She couldn't risk having what happened to her happen to Natalie. 'So we'd have no choice but to go back to the camp. I bet he's waiting for us there!' Ellie wanted to laugh at the irony; they had *wanted* to get back to the camp. Not go further into the darkening trees. He could have just put up a sign! But instead he did *this* to her friend. Damage she would never recover from. Even if Natalie survived, Ellie had seen the state of her leg. She would never use it again.

A crunch from behind made Ellie spin so fast she almost lost her balance from where she was crouched, hammer clutched desperately in both hands, but her heart suddenly sang in relief as she saw Billy approach. He looked tired, stressed, and was clutching a large two by four as defence, but unharmed.

'Ellie! Natalie!' he called out as she approached.

'Billy!' Ellie was on her feet, and rushed, embracing him in a hug that was more than a little awkward, thanks to the two by four. 'Please! Natalie, she's... It's a bear trap! We have to help her!' Ellie gestured to where Natalie was trapped, noticing that the girl had turned so pale she was unsure if she was even aware of what was happening around her anymore.

'Okay, okay. Don't panic. Stay calm.' Billy said quickly, rushing over to bend down beside the bear trap. 'Here, the release is just here. Nice and easy. Hold on.' Ellie couldn't see what Billy was doing, but the trap sprang open, causing Natalie to gasp in pain again, and fall back onto the ground, where she lay, shivering. Ellie rushed towards her.

'W-we need something to stop the bleeding!' she announced, eyes turning to Billy. 'Right? I-I mean, we need to... I dunno, put pressure on it? Wrap it?' Ellie pushed her blood soaked hands onto the spurting wound. It was all around Natalie's leg. What was she meant to do!? She couldn't cover it all. She began to reach for her camp counsellor's shirt, deciding that removing it was her only option, to use that as a bandage.

Ellie paused, looking up at Billy. Why wasn't he helping? He was just standing back, aghast, still clutching the two by four.

'I... I didn't realise it would be so... bad...' he said uneasily. His voice was unsteady as he spoke.

'What... do you mean?' Ellie asked, but she didn't have to. Cold realisation set in. Her entire body felt like it turned to ice. 'Wait. How did you know to disarm the trap so easily?' Ellie wished that she hadn't asked. God, how she wished it. Because the look in Billy's eyes changed.

'I'm really, truly, sorry.' he said, and then he swung the two by four directly at Ellie's face. All she knew after was blackness.

Oddly enough, the first thought that entered Ellie's head was how thirsty she was. Her throat felt like she had gargled ashes. Her eyes opened through a groggy heaviness, and she winced at the light. Her head was throbbing, and her first instinct was to move a hand to it, but as she made a move to do so, she realised that she was restrained. She felt coarse rope bite into her wrists. She tried to force the scene into better focus. She was still alive. Somehow, she was *still alive*.

Opposite her, she could see Natalie, tied tightly to a wooden chair, but unconscious. Or at least, that was what Ellie hoped. She was so pale that she might have been dead. Ellie tried desperately to move across to her, but her hands and legs were tied to their own chair. She looked around desperately, trying to take in where they were. She recognised it. The community hut. She could even see the yellow window frames she was so proud of, revealing the pitch black night outside.

And then she saw Billy, leaning by the door against the wall. His body was taught, as if he was trying to force himself to relax, but having no luck. Ellie glared at him furiously.

'You...' she rasped. Her mouth wasn't gagged. She supposed that was a good start. Her throat was so dry it was hard to form words, but she forced each one out. 'It was... you...' Billy moved from the wall, and let out a hollow sounding laugh.

'Me?' he asked incredulously. 'You saw that thing! You really think that was me? How good do you think my cosplay game is?' he asked mockingly. Ellie looked across at Natalie, down at the bloodied leg, and back at him.

'The traps...' Ellie asked. God, words were so hard to force...

'Okay, yeah, the traps were me. But I was just helping out.' Billy explained, before throwing his hands up. 'I know, I know, you must think I'm evil. But trust me, this is about *family*. This is important.

I'm not doing this for *me*.'

'What... the hell are you talking about?' Ellie asked fiercely. She strained at the ropes. They were tied tightly. Of course. Billy and all his camp leader knowledge. He knew how to tie a knot.

'The story, the legend that Danny told you last night. It's true. But he missed an important detail. The Mirror Monster's youth worker, the one who sent him to the camp, way back '79, eventually she started a family. She had a son.' Billy explained.

'Let me guess. You.' Ellie said bitterly.

'Look, we tried to resolve it all peacefully. We even paid for his burial. We hoped putting him in the ground, near the marsh, would leave him at rest. But it didn't work. Once we realised the Mirror Monster was back, we realised it was only a matter of time before it came back after my mom. So I did what I had to do. I kept guiding people here. I kept making sure it had plenty of *prey*. To keep it away from my mom. As long as he kills a bunch of dumbass teenagers every year, he's happy, and my mom gets to live. Don't you see? I'm doing this for her. I'm a *good son*.'

'The benefactors... The owners that we couldn't meet....?' Ellie questioned.

'My parents, yeah. My mom made a lot of money from writing all about the Mirror Monster's psyche. Easily enough to buy this place, do it up. Of course, we had to recruit local, keep it under the radar, but it wasn't hard to find a bunch of dumb teenagers looking for an excuse to party it up for six weeks.' Billy smiled bitterly.

'They were my friends!' Ellie practically screamed, tears in her eyes.

'Were... your friends?' he repeated, puzzled. 'Oh, I'm sorry? Did you think you were going to be the final girl or something? That you're the one who's going to survive?' Billy paused, and laughed. 'No, there's still two more of them out there. Melissa and Danny, right? Maybe one of them will survive, but not you. You're just another sacrifice for him. Another horny idiot. I saw you drooling over Danny. What, did you take this job so you two could finally be alone? So you could get in his pants? This is what happens to trash like you. You won't be missed. My mom is smart. She's *intelligent*. She deserves to live. You're just a sacrifice. Another dumb bimbo. Nobody will miss you.'

'Screw you!' Ellie practically spat, jolting against the chair. She noticed the air getting colder. Was it her imagination? Or was it the same chill she had felt when the creature was present last time? Could it be... more than just a feeling? A supernatural sign? The real life equivalent of hearing *ki ki ki, ma ma ma* on the soundtrack whenever Jason showed up? She knew her horror movies. She knew what happened when you tried to side with the killers. 'And how does the Mirror Monster feel about *you? Your* help?' she asked, knowing she had to keep him talking.

'Oh, I think we have an understanding.' Billy smiled, and at that moment, the door behind him burst open. Ellie flinched in her seat, and began struggling desperately, because she knew the source. There it stood, the huge, rotting body of the Mirror Monster, moving steadily towards her. 'See?' Billy smiled. But slowly, the Mirror Monster's masked visage turned to face Billy. It raised its sickle. 'No, wait. What are you doing? I brought them to you! I *gave* them to-'

It was as far as Billy got, before the sickle sailed through the air, slicing his head clean off. It flew through the air and splattered against one of the windows, his blood trickling down the yellow frame. This time, Ellie didn't scream.

'You should watch more horror movies. You can *never* control the killer.' she said bitterly as Billy's lifeless corpse slumped to the ground. Slowly, the Mirror Monster adjusted its gaze to Natalie. Ellie began to fight at her bonds again. Dammit. Why did Billy have to be such a *boy scout*? Not in the good, nice way, in the "too damn good at knots" way. The ropes bit at her arms as she struggled, but they wouldn't release her. The Mirror Monster reached Natalie, and paused. The girl still wasn't conscious. Slowly, it made its way over to one of the tables, and picked up one of the paint brushes left resting there from the day's work. It made its way toward her, and then, taking the paint brush handle, jammed it directly into her eye, pushing it with inhuman strength until it emerged from the other side. Then it released her, leaving her corpse to slump in its bonds. Ellie couldn't even scream. She just watched, mouth agape, too terrified, too beaten, to even make a sound. Had this not been for real, had she not been about to die, she'd have appreciated the Mirror Monster obeying slasher movie villain rules, and making sure it found a creative way to kill its next victim. Instead, she could only sob.

The creature lifted the sickle, and began to advance on Ellie. Ellie began struggling more violently, sobbing and struggling, but she was helpless. It was nearly upon her. She closed her eyes in terror.

She felt a gust of air and heard a wet thud. She opened her eyes to see the Mirror Monster stumbling back, arrow embedded in its heart. Her eyes flew to the doorway, and Danny ran in, a bow from the archery range in his hands. She let out a hysterical laugh, followed by a sob as she looked at Natalie's corpse. She had been right. Bow and arrows. The archery range. Their one chance to stop the creature.

'Ellie! Oh my god, Ellie, you're alive!' Danny rushed to her side, quickly working at the knots. As he found that he couldn't undo them, he instead pulled a pocket knife, and cut them, quickly lifting her free. 'Oh god. Natalie. No.' he said, voice quaking, as he saw where she lay.

'A-and Helen. And Sarah.' Ellie practically sobbed, for a moment falling into his arms. Danny shut his eyes and cursed under his breath.

'It ambushed us on our way back in the pick-up truck. It got Gareth, but we got away, me and Melissa...' Ellie got to her feet slowly, trying to find her strength.

'Melissa's alive?' Ellie's heart for a moment allowed some hope, and then she saw Melissa appear in the doorway. She had never seen her wealthy friend looking quite so rough. Her clothes were stained and filthy with mud, her designer sandals were gone off her feet, her face was streaked with mascara stained tears, and her hair was far messier than she had ever allowed any of them to see it. But she was standing there, shivering uneasily, clutching a machete. Ellie's eyes went back to Natalie's corpse. She was right about the bow and arrow, but apparently wrong that they'd never find a machete. The fact she would never, *ever* be able to tell her that almost made Ellie vomit.

'C'mon, let's get out of here.' Danny grabbed Ellie's hand, a gesture that in happier times would have set her heart fluttering, and began to lead her away. Ellie's eyes went back to the fallen creature, an arrow still lodged in its heart. Suddenly, Ellie pulled back against Danny's grip.

'No, wait!' Ellie's voice stopped both Danny and Melissa in their tracks. 'Don't you see? This happens in every horror movie! They take the killer out, then instead of finishing him off, they just run away and let him get back up! If Laurie just finished Michael off after she stabbed him with the needle in *Halloween*, he'd have never gotten back up to get after her!' Danny looked blank, and Melissa just looked angry.

'This isn't a *movie*, Ellie!' she practically screamed.

'But you can't say that thing is human!' Ellie countered, waving a hand at the fallen creature. 'Don't you want to make sure it's dead!?' Melissa seemed to hesitate at this point, but marched back into the cabin.

'Fine! You're right! I *do* kinda wanna kill this thing.' she announced, lifting up her machete. It was a clumsy action, and it was clear that she had no idea how to actually *use* the blade, but Ellie let her approach. Her instinct told her to caution her, to tell her to be careful, in case the killer was faking being down, but that would just be calling on another film trope again, wouldn't it? The supposedly dead killer springing to life as somebody approached it? Melissa was right that this wasn't a movie. But that thing, it was clearly some kind of monster. It wasn't human.

Ellie hesitated too long, however, and Melissa was soon standing over it. She lifted up the machete.

'This is for killing my friends and *ruining my top*!' she cried, and she drove the machete downwards. Ellie didn't even have time to appreciate the blonde's attempt at a one-liner, however, because the Mirror Monster's hand snapped forward, grabbing the machete blade, wrapping its bulbous digits around the weapon. Black blood oozed from its bloated fingers, and Melissa gasped as it effortlessly held the blade back. In one quick motion, it ripped the weapon from Melissa's hands and rose to its feet. Melissa stumbled back and turned to run, but it grabbed her long hair, and hurled her towards the wall. She instead slammed into a window, smashing it with a mighty crash of glass. Ellie watched as her body disappeared into the darkness outside. Dammit! Why hadn't she warned her? She had hesitated! She had known it felt wrong in her gut and now it was too late.

'Quickly! Outside!' Danny yelled, and Ellie didn't hesitate this time, following as slowly the Mirror Monster took the machete from where it was embedded in one hand, and gripped the handle.

Ellie almost collided with Danny as the two burst out into the dark night. It was so dark outside that only the glow from the cabin gave any light at all, and Ellie desperately wished for a flashlight. Rain poured down around them, and thunder rumbled in the sky. In an instant, Ellie was soaked to the skin. The storm somehow seemed appropriate, despite it being the middle of summer. She heard a groan, and immediately raced around the side of the cabin.

'Melissa!' Ellie called out into the darkness, hearing another pained groan. She was alive! She looked in bad shape, covered in cuts and blood from shards of glass, and she seemed to barely be moving from the pain. Ellie figured she was lucky her neck hadn't snapped by how the creature had thrown her, but she was willing to take any luck she could get. She had landed right outside of the window, just beside the propane tank. If the angle had been slightly different, she'd have smashed into the heavy metal tank and no doubt be in even worse shape.

Before Ellie could reach her fallen friend, however, the entire wall of the cabin burst open, the Mirror Monster smashing through the thick, sturdy wood panelling like it was made of cardboard. Ellie threw her hand up to shield her face, feeling the wooden splinters lash at her, her sneakers slipping and skidding on the wet mud. She stopped just in front of the creature, and scrambled back, falling on her backside. The smell of propane gas filled her nostrils, where the Mirror Monster had ruptured the tank. Melissa was trying to scramble away, sobbing, with what little strength she had left. The Mirror Monster swept down and picked Melissa up in one hand, lifting her high. In its free hand, it held the machete, and pulled it back.

'No!' Danny screamed, barrelling past where Ellie had fallen and colliding with the creature. The Mirror Monster didn't even flinch. It was like Danny had run at full speed into a tree trunk. With an almost casual annoyance, it back-handed Danny, sending him flying back, landing on Ellie. Pain shot through Ellie's back as she crashed to the ground, beneath Danny's weight. The two could only watch from where they were a crumpled heap on the ground as the Mirror Monster hoisted Melissa up into the air, and then brought the machete down directly on her head, splitting it in two. One half of her face fell, lop-sided, a dead eye glaring at Ellie. This time, Ellie *did* throw up. She let out a desperate sob. Had it killed Melissa because she had tried to finish it off? On Ellie's suggestion? Had she just gotten yet another one of her friends killed? She had watched so many horror movies, she was supposed to be the *expert*, and still, she couldn't save them! There was nothing she could do. There was no competing with the unstoppable.

Ellie suddenly became aware that she was being hauled to her feet. Danny lifted her up, and started to run, forcing her to have to run to keep up.

'Run, Ellie! Run!' he yelled. Ellie nodded. Nothing else mattered now. It was a case of fight or flight, and they chose flight. 'Melissa's car! It's still back on the road! If we can make it...' Behind them, the Mirror Monster began to chase after them, moving at a steady, walking pace. God, it never ran. Ellie remembered that most of all. How it never *ran*. Just like the movies. Just like those slow lumbering killers. And yet, somehow, it seemed to be keeping up with them. Impossibly, every time Ellie looked behind her as they ran as fast as their legs would carry them, it was only a few feet behind, with that same slow, determined pace, marching after them.

Ellie saw the exit to the camp, the back of the welcome arch visible. They just had to make it down that road. She looked behind her. It felt like the Mirror Monster was falling behind. They were nearly there.

And then she stopped, sliding in the muck, and grasping at Danny's hand.

'The keys!' she suddenly cried.

'Shit!' Danny cursed. 'Melissa-' he cut himself off. He didn't have to say anything else. Of course Melissa had the keys to her car. They both turned around, looking back at the distant light of the cabin. The Mirror Monster was nowhere to be seen.

'It knows.' Ellie somehow knew. She just *knew*. 'It knows we have to come back. It's waiting for us.'

'That's… that's fine. Let it wait. We'll get out of here on foot.' Danny suggested. Ellie was actually a little impressed, despite her terror. It was a pragmatic suggestion. The type of thing protagonists in a horror film never thought to do. 'We just have to make the main road. Flag something down or, hell, walk back into town. I bet it won't follow us to civilisation.'

'It won't work.' Ellie said quietly after a moment. '…You can't outrun it. If we try, it'll come after us.'

'What are you saying?' Danny questioned.

'…It's waiting for us, right?' Ellie replied. 'We know where it is.' Fight or flight. That phrase returned to her head. All night she'd been choosing flight. Time to try the other thing.

'Please tell me you've got a better plan than just trying to *fight* that thing? I shot it in the heart!' Danny exclaimed.

'Did you smell the gas? When it broke through the wall?' Ellie asked quickly. Danny paused.

'The ruptured tank? You're thinking-' he paused, and ran his hand down his face in shock. 'Oh no, no way…'

'We get it inside the cabin. In a controlled space. And then we blow that thing straight to Hell.' Ellie told him. 'Let's see it come back from *that*!' Her voice was determined, but she didn't know if it was courage or pure hysteria at what she had faced that night. She felt like she had no fear left. It was like she had spent it all. Her horror was gone. Now all that was left was a desire for revenge. To hurt that thing like it had hurt her, like it had hurt her *friends*.

'You're actually insane, you know that, right?' Danny asked, before breaking into a smile. 'I think I like it.' Ellie couldn't resist a blush, despite the situation. 'Okay, let's do it.'

'First thing's first, we need matches.' Ellie pointed out.

'Natalie smokes. I bet she has some on her.'

'What!? She told me she quit!' Ellie replied, annoyed for a moment, before realising that there was no more Natalie for her to take her annoyance out on.

'Yeah, she didn't want you to know. Said you were always guilt tripping her.' Danny replied, but his expression said his thoughts had gone to the same place. No more Natalie... Or Helen, or Sarah, or Melissa... It was so horrific it bordered on the surreal. Ellie's brain couldn't quite process that her best friends were actually *gone*.

'So, we go back to the cabin, one of us raids the corpse of one of our dead friends for her keys, the other raids the other corpse for some matches. Yeah. I'm feeling really good about this.' Ellie groaned sarcastically.

'Hey, this was your idea!' Danny reminded her, before looking back at the darkened trail out of the camp. 'We can still run?' he offered. Elle looked at the dirt road, the very same one Melissa's car had become stuck on yesterday, where her journey had began, and shook her head. It was dark, it was long, it was unsafe and Ellie knew from personal experience traipsing down it yesterday that the terrain was badly uneven and mucky. She definitely didn't fancy the idea of trying to make her way down it in the dark. She knew if they ran they'd never make it. They had one choice. Stand and fight.

'And do what?' Ellie asked. 'Say we make it, say we get out of there and somehow that thing doesn't catch us... What, you want to wake up every night, knowing it's still out there? Wake up every night knowing that we had a chance to stop it, and we didn't take it? That a monster murdered our friends and we just let it go and saved ourselves? That every person who ever comes to this cursed place, every person who sees it, every person that thing kills from now on, could have been saved but instead we chose to *run away*?' Danny seemed to pause, looking at her, and smiling.

'Look, dammit, this isn't the time, but damn if you're not hot giving a big speech like that.' he grinned. Ellie felt her face flush and her blood boil. God, she wanted to kiss him, but she fought the urge. Even if there wasn't a killer on the loose, she knew it was ridiculously inappropriate. Their friends were dead! She always thought it was so cheesy and dumb when in horror movies the two lovers would finally kiss among all the death, but in that moment, she understood the desire. The urge. Emotions were running so high, so hot, it was like everything was enhanced. You just wanted to give in to your feelings. But Ellie knew that she couldn't. Not here, not now. 'Alright, let's go.' he nodded. Ellie allowed herself a smile, and began to make her way back towards the community hut.

The hut was the only building with its lights left on in the entire camp. The golden glow that burst out from the windows, as well as the gigantic burst hole in the side from the Mirror Monster's improvised exit, made it look like a beacon, calling them towards it. It only cemented Ellie's belief that it was a trap. That the monster was still there, lurking, waiting for them. But it didn't matter. It was just her and Danny left. Like it or not, she was the final girl now. And when it came to final girls, there was only one of two ways you could go. Either, you were the helpless damsel, having to be saved at the last moment by an outside force, like Laurie in the original *Halloween*, or you fought back and you kicked that monster's ass, like, well, Laurie, in *Halloween*. Except the 2018 one. In retrospect, Ellie was glad she hadn't made that comparision out loud, because it sounded *really dumb*.

The point was, Ellie was ready to fight back. She turned to Danny.

'Okay. You get the keys. I'll go for the matches.' she decided. 'That thing's smashed a hole in the wall. It's given me a way out even if it blocks the door.'

'Wait, you want to go into the cabin? As what, bait?' Danny asked, his tone full of worry.

'I'm the final girl, right? It'll come after me.' Ellie smiled weakly. Danny gave her a look, as if he wanted to argue, as if he wanted to tell her this wasn't a movie, just like everybody had been doing all night, but he didn't say anything. Ellie guessed he knew by now. They were playing by those rules now, no matter how stupid they seemed to be.

'Yeah, well, I look terrible in a bikini, so you better not die. No way in hell I'm being the final girl.' Danny tried to joke lamely. Ellie cracked a weak smile.

'You know, it's pretty much an untrue film trope that the final girl always ends up in something skimpy. Usually-'

'Not the time, Ellie.'

'Right, right, sorry.' Ellie sighed, knowing he was right. The film trivia could wait until later. She wondered if she was stalling intentionally. 'Okay. Let's do this. Let's go.'

Ellie didn't wait. It reminded her of the year before, in better times, when they'd all taken a trip to a lake together. There had been a big rock that they'd dared each other to jump off of. Ellie had just run and leapt, without looking, knowing it was the only way she'd do it. That's what she did now. She leapt without looking. She ran in a sprint as fast as her legs could carry her, lungs burning as anxiety and fear sapped her strength, until she sprinted right through the door of the cabin. She actually crashed into one of the counters that made up the tiny cooking area, unable to stop in time, her rain slick sneakers sliding on the wooden floorboards. She turned, breathing hard. She realised the smart thing to do would have been to have returned to the shed for more weapons first, but it had been too dark. She didn't think they could have found it anyway, and even if they had, there were too many chances for an ambush. She entered the cabin, and immediately noticed that it stank of gas. That was how she knew her plan was going to work. She turned quickly, rushing towards Natalie, her body still tied to the chair, the paintbrush still lodged in her eye. Ellie let out a whimper and fought it back. Oh god, Natalie. She realised if her plan worked, she was going to blow up the body of her closest friend. Scenes flashed across her mind, she pictured herself dressed all in black, at Natalie's funeral, knowing that the coffin was empty because of *her*. She hesitated. Just for the briefest moment, she hesitated.

And then came the sound. It was a sound every horror fan knew. She may have been the least outdoorsy girl in the world, she might have never touched a real garden tool, but she knew *that* sound. The sound of a chainsaw.

Bursting through the doorway behind her, the Mirror Monster stomped towards her, the chainsaw from the shed now in its hand. Plumes of smoke and the smell of gasoline mixed with the propane gas, and for a moment Ellie wondered if there would be a spark from within the chainsaw that would blow them both apart, but nothing came. She was still alive. All Ellie had to do was make sure she stayed that way. How hard could that be? The creature lumbered towards her, bringing the chainsaw down. Ellie leapt backwards, but crashed into the counter behind her. The Mirror Monster brought the chainsaw up as Ellie rolled back across the counter and fell clean on the other side just as it brought the saw down again. It chewed into the counter with a roar, sending shards of wood and splinters flying, slicing into Ellie's face, one leaving a particularly painful cut above her eyebrow. It hauled the chainsaw free, ready to move towards her again, and she realised now she had nowhere to go, trapped in the small kitchenette.

'Get away from her, you bitch!' Danny's voice somehow cut over the roar of the chainsaw. He was stood behind the Mirror Monster, clutching the Monster's very own sickle. He must have found it after the creature dropped it when it was shot with the arrow, she realised. He gave Ellie a grin. 'How was *that* for a horror movie reference?' The Mirror Monster turned, approaching him.

'I wouldn't really count *Aliens* as a "horror movie".' she said with a dorky grin. Danny returned the smile, but then fell deadly serious.

'Get the matches!' Danny yelled quickly as he moved with all the agility he could muster.

Ellie ran as fast as she could, padding down Natalie's shirt. It was damp from her being dragged through the rain, and she discarded a now broken smartphone and a pack of tobacco from her tight jean pockets. No matches. She looked at what was left of Natalie's camp counsellor shirt. There was a pocket on the chest, just where the shirt had been torn in her escape from the shed. Ellie reached inside, closing her eyes and praying.

No matches. Ellie cursed.

'Ellie! Hurry the hell up!' Danny screamed as he turned and ran across the room, trying to put some distance between himself and the whirring chainsaw blade. Ellie realised that maybe the matches had been lost when Natalie fled the shed. Maybe they'd fallen out, and they had no hope left.

No, wait! Ellie remembered seeing Natalie on the roof, stuffing something into her back pocket! Quickly, she pulled Natalie's body forward the best she could, given she was still tied to the chair, just as with a clang she saw the sickle fly out of Danny's hand. Ellie reached inside and pulled the soggy pack of matches free. The Mirror Monster seemed to sense what was happening, and turned on her. With one quick movement, it batted Danny across the face with the flat piece of the chainsaw, knocking him down and fracturing teeth. Danny fell to the floor coughing up blood, but the monster didn't even slow down at all. It hurled the chainsaw to the floor and instead scooped up the sickle. It seemed to want to use its signature weapon to finish Ellie off. She wasted no time, drawing a match and striking it. Nothing. She struck it again and again, but still nothing, until it snapped! She looked up, the creature with its sickle raised. The blade came whistling down.

There was a sickening thud as it impacted, but a moment passed and Ellie realised it wasn't her body it had hit. Danny had thrown himself in front of it, somehow having managed to get to his feet. He turned, eyes wide, blood spluttering from the smashed teeth in his mouth. He wavered, as the creature pulled the sickle back out of him, leaving him to sag to the ground. All Ellie could do was scream. Breathing harder than she ever had before, vomit rising in her stomach, her heart thundering so fast she thought she might have a heart attack then and there, she did the only thing she could think of to do. She grabbed the chair that she had been tied to by Billy earlier that night, and swung it like a club at the Mirror Monster's face. It shattered into splintered wood, and the creature took a step back. It didn't seem hurt, but its mask had been dislodged, and it desperately tried to work it back into position. There was no time to waste. She threw herself under Danny's arm pit and ran for the hole in the wall the Mirror Monster had made earlier. She struggled with his weight and their options, but she had the second match in her hands. One strike. Nothing. Two strikes, nothing. Three and-

A flame! She threw it backwards into the gas filled cabin just as she reached the hole in the wall, and the cabin exploded with a mighty roar. She was flung forwards, sailing through the air, losing her grip on Danny. She felt the skin on her back burn, the flesh tighten and wrinkle as it cooked and her clothes melted into it, incredible pain snaking across her back like the sudden cracking of a pane of glass, she felt the sting of debris and her entire body jolt, her joints rattled, as she crashed to the wet ground, rolling forcefully as bones crunched and her body bruised.

And then there was nothing but silence. The hut burned. The rain seemed to have stopped. All she could feel was the immense heat upon her face. She heard a cough, and her eyes fell to Danny beside her. He was *alive*! He was actually alive! She ran to his side, unable to find the words, sobbing in relief. Her relief began to turn to horror as she looked at him. That sickle wound was so deep, and he had caught the blast a lot worse than she had. He was badly burned. She fought back tears. She struggled, putting her entire body under one of his arms to lift him up. Against all belief, Danny managed to stand, his legs shaking. He stared into the burning flames.

'It's over. It's finally over.' he breathed a shaky sigh of relief.

And maybe that's where the story would have ended for Ellie Cartwright, had Danny not said what he did next. Maybe Ellie and Danny would have been the lone survivors of a massacre, and that would have been it. They'd have gotten on with their lives. But then Danny said one more thing.

'Nothing could have survived that.' And just like that, the world shifted. Reality changed. Because there was a golden rule. A rule that Ellie should have known. A rule that said if you had definitely killed the monster, if you had destroyed it beyond any doubt, if there was *absolutely* no way it could have survived that, then it had definitely survived that.

Danny spoke those fateful words, and reality changed. But what happened next, the return of the Mirror Monster, Ellie's journey afterwards, meeting Suzi and Nina, forming The Last Girls Standing, fighting ghosts, gremlins and monsters from beyond, was another story for another time. Standing there, bloodied and beaten, watching the cabin burn, wasn't the end for Ellie. It was beginning.

THE STORY IS CONTINUED IN:
THE LAST GIRLS STANDING

ALSO AVAILABLE

**A SUMMER CAMP. AN UNDEAD KILLER.
A FINAL GIRL. YOU MIGHT THINK YOU
KNOW THIS STORY. THINK AGAIN...**

Ellie Cartwright is the lone survivor of the
St. Mary's Marsh massacre. That's not how
her story ends. It's how it begins.

Because Ellie's not the only girl to have
faced evil and survived. There are others.
And now, they've sworn to protect those in
danger. They've sworn to fight back against
the creatures that lurk in the darkness.

They are the Last Girls Standing.

And Ellie's journey is just getting started...

SURVIVING WAS JUST THE BEGINNING...

T.L.G.S. HOME VIDEO presents...

Surviving was just the start...

HORROR

COMEDY

THE LAST GIRLS STANDING

L.C. Valentine

EX-RENTAL ONLY

VHS